Joyful Saturday: Marie's Bat Mitzvah

Written by
Donna Wallace-Harmon
Illustrated by
Nadee dewakara Hewage

ISBN 978-1-7387716-1-5

Book Cover, Book Designer and Illustrator
Nadee dewakara Hewage

FOREWORD

My grandma, Mabel Violet Morales Curtis, was a Baptist Christian, who sang in the church choir, and was a great home cook. She was very proper; always well dressed and wore makeup and pearls every day. Born in 1910, she was the last child in a mixed-race family of Black and Jewish descendants. She married at age 30, and was widowed at age 51. She lived her life for her children and grandchildren. Grandma Curtis died in her 71st year, six months before her birthday.

I was always intrigued by many factors of our family history. After our grandma passed away, I learned more about her family heritage. We found out her ancestors were from Portugal and Spain, who fled for their lives because of discrimination against the Jews. I was fascinated and wanted to learn more about my heritage which had never been told to us as children. I love reading, watching, and hearing about history, especially my own.

I have learned that In Judaism, it is the tradition to celebrate children coming of age, whether one is Orthodox or Reform Jew. They both celebrate Bat Mitzvah and Bar Mitzvah, to be reminded of their faith, culture, and tradition.

Dedication

Dedicated to my Savta/Grandma Mabel Violet Morales Curtis.
My Grandma was my inspiration, I enjoyed being with her.
I love listening to her sing, and seeing her generosity to
our neighbours.

Glossary:

Hebrew word Ima – mother

Hebrew word Savta – grandmother/grandma

Hebrew word Ahavasheli/Ahuvasheli – sweetie

Hebrew word Abba – father

Hebrew word Saba – grandfather/grandpa

Hebrew word Tallit–   prayer shawl

Hebrew word Yamulke– kippah or skullcap

Hebrew word–Tefellin– boxes which contain scrolls

Hebrew word – Bat Mitzvah– A 13-year-old girl coming of
age celebration

Hebrew word – Bar Mitzvah– A 13-year-old boy coming of
age celebration

Hebrew word – Rugelach – Yiddish little twist pastry filled with
cream cheese, or sour cream, nuts, fruit jams, sugar,
cinnamon, and raisins.

Joyful Saturday:
Marie's Bat Mitzvah

Donna Wallace-Harmon

W T F S S
9 10 11 12 13 14
16 17 18 19 20 21
23 24 25 26 27 28
29 30

Joyful Saturday: Marie's Bat Mitzvah

Marie was so excited! Next Saturday evening, she would celebrate her Bat Mitzvah and she could hardly wait! But as she thought more about it, she frowned. Her brother Mario would also be celebrating his Bar Mitzvah on the same day, and she was not happy about that.

Marie and Mario were twins, and they did everything together. Usually, Marie loved doing things with her brother, but she wanted her special day all to herself. She tried to talk to her older sister Evelyn about it.

"I want to read the Torah all by myself. I don't want Mario to help me. Everyone knows he can read really well, but I've been practicing!" Marie explained.

"And Saba/Zayde (grandpa) Albert is going to be the Rabbi to conduct the ceremony, and I really want to make him proud."

"I thought you said reading was boring and you didn't like it?" Evelyn asked.
Marie got upset.

"I've been trying really hard! I practice it as much as my art and music. Remember I didn't like sewing at first? But Ima (Mum) and Savta (Grandma) helped me sew my own dress for my Bat Mitzvah!" Marie said. But Evelyn just shrugged, and went back to talking on her phone.

Next, Marie decided to talk to Mario about her feelings.

"Mario, is it okay for me to celebrate my Bat Mitzvah all by my self?" Marie asked. Mario looked surprised. "Why? I thought we were a team?" he asked.

"Yes we are, but this time I want to do something just for me," she explained. Mario scratched his head as he thought about it and then he said "Sure. If Mum and Dad say yes, let's give it a try." But he didn't look happy, because he wanted to celebrate with Marie.

Marie tried for days to get her parents to listen to her, but instead she grew more and more frustrated. She tried talking to her Savta (grandma) and Ima (mother), as she helped them prepare for the big day. While they baked brownies, and cooked salmon, Marie did her best to convince them that she should read the Torah by herself.

"I've been practicing day and night! I know how to pronounce all the words, and I understand their meaning. I don't need Mario to help me," she explained. Her grandmother's eyes twinkled as she listened to Marie.

"But Marie, think of all your family who will be there. All your cousins are coming and your friends from school, and it will be such a treat for them to see you read together. The bond of family is most important Ahuvasheli/Bubbelah (sweetie)," Grandma

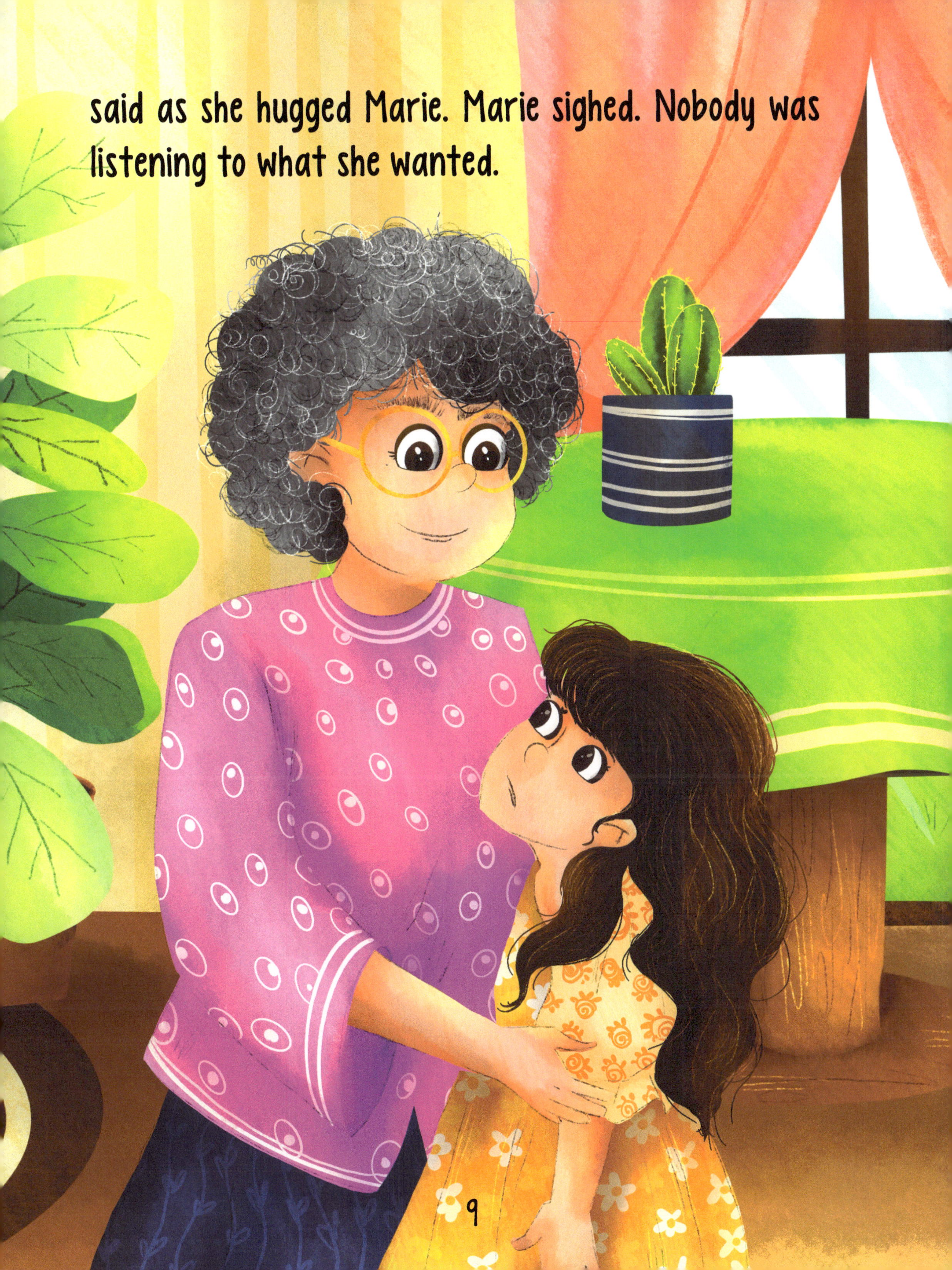

said as she hugged Marie. Marie sighed. Nobody was listening to what she wanted.

She tried talking to her father as she helped clean and decorate the hall for the celebration.

"Abba/Tati (Dad), I'm my own person. I want to have my own Bat Mitzvah. I don't want to do everything with Mario anymore," Marie said.

"You only get one Bat Mitzvah Marie. Do you really want to celebrate it without the person you are closest to in the world? The love of the Messiah is first, the love of family is second. Think about it", he said.

Marie's face grew hot and she wiped angry tears from her eyes. Why didn't anyone understand her?

On Friday afternoon, Marie sat in her room still feeling upset. She suddenly smelled the delicious scent of hot Rugelach coming from the kitchen. She ran downstairs, and saw her family gathered around the kitchen table, laughing, and talking about the upcoming celebration on Saturday. She stood at the door, hesitant to enter.

"Her abba(dad) saw her standing by the door and smiled. "Come sit with us Ahuvasheli/bubbelah (sweetie)."

Marie came in and sat beside Savta(grandma), at the kitchen table. Her mouth watered as she looked at the steaming Rugelach but she didn't take any.

Her Abba (Dad) said, "It looks like something is bothering you. Can we talk about it?"

Marie said, "I would like to read the Torah aloud on Saturday by myself. I know I always ask Mario for help with my homework, but I can really do this on my own. Nobody believes me."

Abba(dad) said, "Marie we are your family. We care about each other very deeply and want all you kids to succeed. If you want to read the Torah to us at your Bat Mitzvah, it's your decision. We believe in you, and love you.

On Saturday morning, Marie opened her eyes and sat up straight in bed. It's today! She thought, as she rushed to the shower, curled her hair, had breakfast, and got dressed in her beautiful cobalt blue dress – the color of the deep sea. At 9:30 am, the whole family walked to the synagogue for 10:00 am service. They got there early, took their seats and waited patiently for Rabbi grandpa Albert to give instructions to Marie and Mario.

Marie was so nervous she could barely sit still as the service began.

Today is my day! She thought as she felt her heart thumping. Today I will make promises to the Messiah, my family, friends, and to the whole world.

At that moment, Grandpa Albert looked at the twins and smiled. He called their names and asked them to come up to the altar.

Marie felt her palms grow damp. Suddenly her legs felt shaky and she was trembling. "I can do this...I can do this!" She encouraged herself as tears began to sting her eyes.

I'm an adult now. I can think for myself and I can read the Torah by myself!

She and Mario put on each other's tallit. Mario wore his yarmulke and grandpa put on Mario's tefillin. Then she and Mario walked up to the altar together. Marie went up to the podium first, while Mario followed her. She looked back at him, and he smiled at her.

"Please read for both of us Marie. I know you can do it. We can stand together," Mario said.

Marie hugged him tightly. Taking a deep breath, Marie read the holy words of the Torah, in a clear, loud voice. She did not make one mistake. When she had finished, everyone cheered!

I did it! She thought as she and Mario hugged again. But the day was not over yet. When they got home, their grandparents surprised them with new clothes for the celebration dinner.

That evening, all the family and friends gathered in the hall for the celebration dinner. Marie felt like a queen in her new dress, as she and Mario proceeded into the hall with their family.   Grandpa Albert blessed the occasion, then said, "Let's eat!" Marie ate, drank, danced, received gifts, and had great fun with Mario until she was exhausted.

Much later as she lay in bed, she smiled to herself. She loved her twin, but now she truly felt like her own person.

"Tomorrow, I begin a new chapter in my life," she thought as she drifted off to sleep.